I0648914

Eyre Crowe

Thackeray's Haunts and Homes

Eyre Crowe

Thackeray's Haunts and Homes

ISBN/EAN: 9783337278960

Printed in Europe, USA, Canada, Australia, Japan

Cover: Foto ©Andreas Hilbeck / pixelio.de

More available books at **www.hansebooks.com**

Thackeray's Haunts and Homes

Thackeray's Haunts and Homes

By

Eyre Crowe, A. R. A.

With Illustrations from
Sketches by the Author

New York
Charles Scribner's Sons
1897

Illustrations

vii

Illustrations

Entrance Hall of House at No. 13 Great
Coram Street.

Thackeray's Haunts and Homes

THACKERAY struck the true keynote, as regards the surroundings of the illustrious among us, when he said, in one of his "Roundabout Papers" of the year 1860: "We all want to know details regarding men who have achieved famous feats, whether of war, or wit, or eloquence, or knowledge." Wit, eloquence, and knowledge may fairly be said to be comprised in the compass of his literary powers. While, therefore, it is still possible to do so, I have undertaken to garner a sheaf of sketches giving the outward look of his habitations, before the inevitable house-wrecker sweeps away these literary vestiges. As he has pointed out, a few

1

rough strokes of the pencil will be more helpful in this respect than the most elaborate descriptive sentences can be. While following in approximate chronological sequence the connecting-links, omitting the Charterhouse School, which has been ably illustrated before, I give, without further comment, the sketches, worked out *in situ*.

Thackeray's first tentative effort at the mastery of a liberal profession was that of becoming a pupil of a special pleader, then the recognized method of mastering the intricacies of legal practice, since gone out of date. He chose a successful master of the craft, Taprell, and enrolled himself as pupil. His chambers were on the ground floor of No. 1 Hare Court.

Through the courtesy of Mr. Shackleton Hallett and Mr. William T. Raymond, the present tenants of Taprell's chambers at

Taprell's Chambers, No. 1 Hare Court, Temple, where Thackeray
studied law in 1832.

No. 1 Hare Court, I was allowed to make the sketch here given. It enables one to realize the scene of the grateful pupil's endeavors to master the intricacies of law, as he sat in that same room upward of sixty years ago; staying till nigh six o'clock in the afternoons with his master. The panel-oak wainscot, into which numerous book-shelves are inserted, holding convenient folios for reference in search of precedents, is still here, helping the thick brick walls, which withstood the Great Fire of London, further to deaden all sounds but that of the postman's knock on the oaken door. It is whispered that in former days, "after office hours in the evening," much merriment, including dancing, took place in this capacious apartment. The guitar, which may be noticed ensconced in a top-shelf recess, reminds one of the old Queen Anne days, as recorded in Dick Steele's "Spectator," when the music-

5

ally inclined barrister used to wake the Temple echoes with the sonorous hautboy, ending by piteous appeals to the Benchers to stop the noise. Briefs, bound with official red tape, strew the tables, at which you notice the most comfortable arm-chairs, inviting careful perusal. This is in accordance with modern ideas of comfort and with the dignity of the legal aspirant; but in Thackeray's letters he seems to dwell with semi-splenetic humor on the fact that backs to seats were not encouraged in his days. In a letter to his mother he sketched himself as sitting on a high stool; he adds, "the high stools do not blossom and bring forth buds"—in Taprell's chambers. He had his own residential chambers, I believe, in Hare Court, but he probably shared them with another, as did Pendennis with Warrington; so his name doesn't appear in the Taprell list of residents in 1831–32. The glimpse through the win-

Interior of Taprell's Chambers, No. 1 Hare Court, Temple.

dows shows the chambers of Pump Court, which in summer-time are screened from sight by the green leafage.

He soon left Hare Court altogether, and bid good-by to wig and gown for student days in Paris. His biographers say he lived in the Latin Quarter.

The actual atelier in which Thackeray worked in Paris is at present only to be guessed at. In his admirable paper on the "French School of Painting," first published in "Fraser," and afterward incorporated in his "French Sketch Book," he says: "There are a dozen excellent schools in which a lad may enter here, and under the eye of a practised master learn the apprenticeship of his art at an expense of about ten pounds a year." The tradition is that he joined the ranks of Gros' atelier, the nursery of many famous painters. When David was banished from France, as his favorite pupil Gros continued his work and maintained his master's traditions. He came every morning at nine o'clock, and remained for two hours giving loud viva voce hints, so that what was a lesson to one became the property of the remainder, thus multiplying daily, for the benefit of all, his individually applied remarks.

One rule, however, was insisted upon at the outset. This was to copy in chalk a study from the antique, the work of Gros himself as a student in Rome,— the copy to be worked out in one sitting. This was the representation of " Ajax lifting the Body of Patroclus."

One can fancy the grim sense of irony suffusing the features of the great Titmarsh, who, in many passages, has derided this academical practice as time wasted, when invited to fulfil this uncongenial task. Be this as it may, he wrote to his kind mother: " I

go to the atelier steadily every day," and a
cheery note to say he felt he was improving
in his practice.

He describes, in the above-mentioned es-
say, " the score of companions he met with,
all merry and poor, working in a cloud of
smoke, amid a din of puns and a choice
French slang and a roar of choruses, of which
no one can form an idea who has not been
present at such an assembly."

How vivid this is!—and it is true to this
day. The modest pay remains at the same
low figure; but the master visits the school
at rarer intervals; the modern notion being
that the pupil is best left more to his own resources, aided, it may be, by kindly advice
from his co-workers when nonplussed in his
endeavors. Gros' atelier, it may be added,
was situated, at that date, in the inner court
of the Institute, the entrance to it being next
to that of the Mazarin Library, familiar to

most art-lovers as containing the famous small sketch-books of Leonardo da Vinci, as well as the almost anatomical sculptural figure of Voltaire by Pigalle, which so scandalized Voltaire's admirers as a questionable tribute of affection to their yet living philosopher and friend.

The class hours were from eight o'clock in the morning till one in the afternoon. After a brief interval for lunch, throwing off the atelier blouse, the students, then as now, crossed the Bridge of Arts, and wound up the day with practice in copying the old masters in the Louvre Gallery. Here it was, in the waning hours of the summer noon, that I recollect seeing Thackeray making very deft and pretty water-sketches, alike from the Dutch and French masters.

In the "Edinburgh Review" for January, 1848, appeared a review of "Vanity Fair." The article was written by Mr. Hayward, and

Private Atelier of Baron Gros, Paris, 1834.

Drawn from a print.

states that "he remembered ten or twelve years ago finding Thackeray day after day engaged in copying pictures in the Louvre, in order to qualify himself for his profession." The time mentioned should have been put earlier by two or three years, as he was writing for the "Constitutional" up to July, 1837, having married, and given up the brush practice, with a view to a profession, a year before that time.

Thackeray's common-sense was manifested here by the fact that his copies were not the usual lengthy ponderings over one canvas, with the comparatively tedious superposition of coats of oil paint one on top of the other, but rapid seizure in water-colors, and in small compass, of the salient features of the old masters before the eye became dulled by labored effort. He shifted his easel often, and really took in a great store of art knowledge of effects, of schemes, of composition, and an insight into technique, giving him wonderful advantage when he enlisted his keen perceptive powers in art criticism. The peaked wide-awake hat, the long, disheveled hair, and the attire of painters at this time gave him capital bits of character to study from, and were pictorial digressions he largely indulged in.

It was in August, 1836, that Thackeray was married to Miss Shawe, at the British Embassy, by Bishop Luscombe, who was chaplain there. He took apartments for himself and his wife in the Rue Neuve St. Augustin there. He was then correspondent of the "Constitutional," and a reference to its columns at this date shows Titmarsh as a most violent anti-Louis-Philippist. I give a sketch of the exterior of the street, though unable to point with exactness to which of the two structures was the real abode, whether the one on the extreme left, to

Rue Neuve St. Augustin, Paris, A. D. 1836.

which I incline, or that next to it. My
apology must be the great length of time
since then — half a century ago. Still vivid,
however, is the impression of the charming
grace and modesty of the hostess, who was
lithe in figure, with hair of the tinge Titian
was so fond of depicting, bordering on red-
ness. This pleasant time of newly married
folks, which is so touchingly found hinted at
with delicate hand in the " Bouillabaisse "
ballad, has not been chronicled in the short
lives of the author hitherto published. The
day's work over, they would stroll off by the
arched entrance, and through that lively
thronged Passage Choiseul, at the far end of
which they would emerge on the street of
the Little Fields. At No. 16 was the now
immortalized restaurateur. I find in the old
Paris guide-book of that date: " Terré
Jeune, Restaurateur; house noted for Span-
ish dishes, and for good wines, and more

especially for the Marseilles dish, 'Bouillabaisse.'" Those curious as to its exact ingredients will find them enumerated in Larousse's dictionary — some of them so scarce as to require a journey to Marseilles itself.

Some months passed, when I recollect frequently having the privilege of meeting the gentle and modest wife of Thackeray. She could sketch, too, but the brimming humor of Thackeray's pencil caused us, in boyish selfishness, to look preferably over his shoulders whenever he took a fancy to evolve pictorial drolleries on paper. The " Constitutional" having ceased to exist as a newspaper, and Paris correspondence lapsing in consequence, Thackeray and his wife left for England. They settled again at No. 18 Albion Street, Hyde Park, for a brief while. Here, it may be mentioned, was born Mrs. Richmond Ritchie, their eldest daughter.

Thackeray's House at No. 18 Albion Street, Hyde Park.

The unpretending house has therefore a double interest as their home, first, and secondly, as the nursery of two generations of romance writers.

Forsaking Tyburnia and leasing a new residence at No. 13 Great Coram Street, Brunswick Square, Thackeray found himself anchored in London for about four years. My visit there in the early part of 1839 was one of the delights of this boyish time. He had ample store of portfolios full of sketches made in Paris, and would, to my great amusement, lend me whichever I chose to carry off and copy. I had come to stay with Andrew Doyle, of the "Morning Chronicle," afterward its editor, who kindly asked me over to see London life. With Doyle I used to spend some pleasant moments at the prandial hour here; Mrs. Thackeray, having our welfare at heart, was quite delightful at her own fireside. Thackeray talked of possible contributions of his own to the "Chronicle," at that time a power in the land, under Black's editorship. But the sentences which caught my juvenile ear were Thackeray's noble acknowledgment of the great powers of "Boz," whose nom de plume covered the walls of London at that time. Without acerbity, but as plain matter-of-fact, Thackeray added plaintively, "he sells thousands of copies to my small hundreds." If the remembrance of the house is connected with the sprightly, cheerful time I now speak of, the present aspect of it causes a melancholy revulsion of feeling. In former days John, the red-breeched butler, used to usher you to warm welcome and good cheer; he was the old retainer of whom so much has been said, who found a niche in a vignette of Pendennis, where he is seen hugging a basket of Madeira with a grin suggestive of mirth to come. He opened the parlor door, which

Thackeray's Residence at No. 13 Great Coram Street, Brunswick
Square, from 1837 to 1840.

has a gentle elliptical turn just to avoid the
angle of the room. (See vignette facing
page 1.) There it is to this day. The house
now is parceled out into lodgings, the door
has a weather-worn aspect, the area is full of
waifs blown in by the gusts and not removed,
even the railing requires adventitious suste-
nance of wire ties. As I sit on the stairs
sketching the hall I ask the friendly inter-
locutor looking over me the cause of the
general aspect of decrepitude of this tene-
ment and that of its companions. He an-
swers that a murder next door, about twenty
years ago, has acted as a spell on the place,
which has not survived the ban. This brings
back to one the wonderful description Thackeray has given in " Fraser " of the night spent
in this very house in July, 1840, as he tossed on
his pillow, thinking all night of the wretch
Courvoisier, the Swiss valet, whose exit is
described in " Going to See a Man Hanged."

Of course the lodging-houses of Margate, whither Thackeray went in the later summer months of 1840 in search of fresh air, are delightful when peopled with the vivacious characters which have been assembled in the wonderful "Shabby Genteel Story," written there at this time. Hence, therefore, the characteristic appearance of one out of numberless specimens of the same type and construction may suffice. But how vapid they look! In the absence of Fitch, the h-dropping painter we get so fond of in spite of this blank in his vocabulary, or the widow Carrickfergus, Thackeray's lodgings are untraceable; they may be demolished — as is also the little arbor, three miles out, where he ensconced himself to write his review of Fielding's works, which appeared in "The Times."

For reasons which need not here be told, as they are well known, the family home

A Typical Margate Lodging and Boarding House.

was now broken up, and Thackeray spent
the coming winter months of 1840 in Paris.
He used to stroll into the Louvre, where I
often saw him in this year, although he had
dropped the pencil and brush for mere copying purposes. At the close of it came the
exciting time causing much preliminary speculation, when the remains of Napoleon I
were brought back to Paris. Of course every
one has read the stirring account Thackeray
gave of this "Second Funeral of Napoleon."
The small sale of that effusion, which was
coupled with the "Chronicle of the Drum,"
was always to me a matter of surprise; as
great as my wonderment, on seeing an original copy of its first edition, to discover it
only measured 4 by 6½ inches. On this famous 19th of December I did not accompany
him to the interior of the Invalides church,
but I stood on one of the numerous sloping
platforms, to which you were admitted by

privileged tickets. They commanded a full
view of the line of procession from the Quai
to the church itself. Two salient facts domi-
nate his graphic description of the pageant
— first, the intensity of the cold inside the
noble fane; and the mastery of hunger over
the usual proprieties in a church. The cold
I can vouch for, as I felt it when pinned
motionless for such a length of time in the
open air. My companion had the laudable
foresight to carry a mysterious handbag with
him from the Hôtel Mirabeau (the "Mira-
bew" of James Delapluche), which was a
source of speculation as to its contents all
that morning. But at the appointed time
he told me to squat down on the floor, upon
which he spread and carved a chicken; that,
and a gulp of sherry from a flask, made us
objects which no doubt would have been
coupled with the groups of hungry soldiery,
emptying their pouches of provender, as

chronicled in Thackeray's letters to Miss
Smith on the same occasion.

Thus fortified, in spite of deprecatory
glances from less fortunate wights near us,
we presently saw a general stir in the crowd,
and heard cries of "Vive la vieille garde";
Polish lancers, Roustam, Napoleon's Mame-
luke orderly, who had survived for the occasion, naval and military dignitaries, kept fil-
ing between the rows of National Guards,
till at last the beflagged monument of gold
and velvet, the catafalque, topped by the
Napoleonic sarcophagus, came in sight, and
as soon had passed out of view, as it was
brought into the church, there to join the
remains of the other great French warrior,
Marshal Turenne.

At four the whole pageant was over, and
the dispersing crowds gave way to mingled
admiration and jeering comments at the life-
sized plaster-casts of imperial heroes lining

the road of march, some sculptors having
nearly come up to the occasion, others the
reverse. Of the whole series, as far as memory serves, only one figure, the dominant
one of that day, the bronze effigy of Napoleon I, by Baron Bosio, has been preserved
to us. It stood at the end of the Invalides
esplanade, and a short time afterward was
hoisted up to the top of the column on the
Boulogne cliffs.

The veteran whose achievements dwell
uppermost in the memory of English so-
journers at Boulogne is Colonel Newcome.
Thackeray, while evolving this noble figure
in his mind, dwelt in an old château called
Brequerecque, which lies on the outskirts of
the town, pleasantly nestled in trees and
shrubberies, and surrounded by a wall high
enough to screen it from the gaze of the pro-
fane public without. The resources of the
furnishing part of it seem to have been

Château de Brequerecque, Boulogne-sur-Mer.— 1854

somewhat scanty, as Thackeray complained, when paying a visit to Dickens, living the same year at the Villa du Camp de Droite —close to Napoleon's Column — that the landlord, a baron, had only allowed one milk-jug as sufficient crockery for the whole establishment.

Like Pendennis, Thackeray used to make the Hôtel des Bains his headquarters. He liked to peer out from any one of its fifty windows looking toward the bustling Quai, watching the groups of fishing-folk, wistfully looking at the smoking steamer's funnels, and, packing up his traps, would go off to his equally liked quarters at the Folkestone Pavilion. The latter had the great advantage of being so near his home; he could go and return, interview his publisher, revise his proofs, and then seek the restful nook over placid seas once more.

In 1842 Thackeray went to Ireland. His

book is still an admirable guide to the Emerald Isle, affording at once a helping descriptive comment by a shrewd observer on places seen, and a means of testing the great improvements which have taken place during the lapse of half a century.

We take the train to Belfast, and without stopping go on to Newtown-Limavaddy, and the first anxious search is to find the home of " Peg," the humble bait-house immortalized by Thackeray. Here is the cheery interior, with the simmering pot of murphies and the indwellers, as the wonderful verses described — drawn by him who pens these lines, who must record his delight at the discovery of this country tap-room quite unchanged (see Frontispiece).

Thackeray, in the " Sketch-Book," revels in the beauties of Glengariff. Here is the etching of the cheery Eccles's Hotel. The

Hôtel des Bains, Boulogne-sur-Mer.   Entrance in Rue Victor Hugo.

views from the windows are a delight, as you
look out on the island-dotted bay.

Thackeray's footsteps bring us to his next
book of travels, in the East. Whilst writing
its finishing chapters, on his way homeward,
at Rome, Thackeray wrote his ballad " The
Three Sailors of Bristol City," to be found
in Mr. Samuel Bevan's discursive " Sand and
Canvas." That author sent Thackeray a
rough copy of these verses, asking permission to publish them in his book. With his
astonishing *bonhomie* and anxiety to humor
a friend's wish, Titmarsh consented, repairing
the vocabulary where faulty, and making a
present of what is the gem of that work.
This was not done without a feeling of com-
punction, as may be gathered from an excla-
mation of his, blurted out to me to this
effect: " He might just as well have let me
publish the verses myself, when I should

have pocketed the fiver, to which I felt en-
titled." The generosity was genuine; the
lament whispered in mock gravity.

Not liking to perform the slow task of
transferring his intended illustrations of East-
ern life, which were to be woven with the
text, on to the wood-blocks for the cuts, he
confided the task to me. I used to go early
in the morning, and to work away under his
directions in his Jermyn Street lodgings. I
had nearly finished the whole set, when a
sudden happy thought struck the author: he
would have his own portrait drawn to be
placed upon the book cover. He pulled out
from a drawer a bright new costume he had
purchased at Cairo, and soon appeared in full
Oriental garb. With the red fez cap and
blue tassel on his head, a crimson silk caftan
round his body, and sleeves pendent, baggy
breeks and red papouche slippers, he ensconced himself on a low divan, grasping a

Eccles's Hotel, Glengariff.

See "Irish Sketch Book," Chapter IX.

long cherry stick, and, crossing his legs, sat immovable till I had finished my outline.

Father Prout happening to call, Thackeray, still thus attired, pulled out a portion of his MS., and read out to us " The White Squall." The last lines, expressed with tearful accents, elicited a subdued but sincere, " That 'll do," from Mahony.

Soon divesting himself of his grand Cairo costume, Thackeray asked us to go with him and have a look at his new chambers, which he had just taken at No. 88 St. James's Street. We did so, and we found these more spacious, airy, and brighter than those he was leaving. Mr. Rideing, in his pleasant, gossipy pages called " Thackeray's London," has adopted the statement, first made in " Thackerayana," that the house has been pulled down since. This is premature; the house, on the contrary, stands secure enough. The post-office is on the ground floor; men of letters are all over the place, not to mention the immediate vicinity haunted by ghosts of these ; next door used to be the St. James's Coffee House, where Swift wrote his " Stella " correspondence ; Gibbon died a few doors off; Theodore Hook used to issue from his house in Cleveland Row to go into Clubland; and so the air seems a genial one for wits.

Very quiet and restful were these chambers. Besides original authorship, Thackeray undertook the sub-editorial business of the " Examiner," consisting mainly in scissoring clippings from the daily papers, which then strewed the floor. Here Thackeray wrote his amusing note to Macvey Napier, editor of the " Edinburgh Review," protesting against his too liberal use of the shears when cutting out well-pondered jokes of Titmarshian humor.

Thackeray next removed to No. 13 Young

Thackeray's Home at No. 13 Young Street, Kensington, from 1846 to 1853.

Street, Kensington (rechristened now No.
16). His family came over from Paris to
keep house for him. His Boston friend, Mr.
James T. Fields, has given an amusing account of his first visit to it, when Thackeray
playfully told him to go down on his knees,
as " Vanity Fair" was written there. My
first glimpse of the structure was before this
time, on his taking possession, and when that
famous book was still in embryo. On turn-
ing to the left, coming from a walk along
the Park, out of High Street, into Young
Street, and suddenly catching sight of the
two bulging half-towers which flank the central doorway, he thought the house had the
air of a feudal castle, and exclaimed, "I 'll
have a flagstaff put over the coping of the
wall, and I 'll hoist a standard up when I 'm
at home!"

It is needless to describe in detail the interior arrangements of this household. The

study has been made the subject of pictorial treatment by Ward, R. A. Some little time back the kindly tenants of the house, Mr. O'Neil, the well-known painter, and his wife, allowed me to renew my old impressions of the place. The first floor bedroom, where Thackeray lay dictating "Esmond" all day, while whiffing his cigar, had been enlarged with the window for a studio; otherwise it was scarcely altered.

I might recall the strange imbroglio caused by an irate gentleman who, fancying a relative had been maligned in some satirical description, sent to Thackeray to come over and settle the business; else he threatened to castigate him publicly. In pursuit of revenge he wrote that he had taken a room opposite, and that he would await Thackeray's arrival on a certain day and hour. The appointment to meet him was made. On that day Thackeray thought fit to take the

precautionary measure of inviting a brawny-
armed artist, Alexander Christie, Head Master
of the Edinburgh School of Design, an ever-
welcome boon companion, as well as myself,
to assist at the meeting so far as to be on
the watch for fisticuffs, should matters come to
that pass. Presently Thackeray rose up from
the dinner-table, armed himself with a small
rattan stick, and walked across the street.
Christie rapidly divested himself of his coat,
tucked up his sleeves,— revealing, I was glad
to note, a good biceps,—and looking anxi-
ously out of the front bay-window, squared
his elbows and clenched his fists in true
pugilistic trim, ready for the signal to rush
across. I did the same. After awhile, to
our relief, we noticed our host emerging
from the doorway unscathed, cool, and erect.
What had happened? we inquired. He re-
plied that he at first found the gentleman in
a state of suppressed fury, thinking some

relative of his had been slandered, and he wanted reparation. Thackeray seems to have proved easily the groundlessness of the charge to his opponent's satisfaction. So the matter ended, without indiscreet divulging of any names. In Anthony Trollope's "Life" of our friend, he fastens the incident upon the quaint Hibernian mixing up of Catherine Hayes, the famous singer, with the character of the murderess of the same name whom Thackeray wrote about. But that story, as told by the supposititious Ikey Solomons, Esq., Jr., appeared more than half a dozen years before this time; the solution must be traced to the license often taken by the romance writer, rather than to possible history.

Besides works of comparatively slow growth he produced the weekly lucubrations for "Punch's" pages, which charm as a rule by their natural ease, suggestive of sponta-

neous rapid conception. That this was not
always the case was once made clear, when
at the appointed time for collecting manu-
script, the printer's boy was announced and
was told to wait in the hall. Thackeray,
pacing the room in which the brain-cudgel-
ing was taking place, exclaimed: "Well,
I must be funny in five minutes." With
pluck he sat down at his desk and shortly
after the printer's devil was off with the
needed copy.

"The Snobs of England, by One of Them-
selves," papers which appeared in the same
favorite periodical, were not thrown off with
any such perfunctory despatch, and week
after week they were clutched at with avid-
ity from February, 1846, to the same month
in 1847. When they were completed and
were on the point of issue as a separate volume, Thackeray, ever on the alert for an ap-
propriate dedicatory preface, thought of his

old friend, W. G. Lettsom, whom he had known as Embassy Attaché at Weimar, Munich, and other places. It was, however, owing to earlier association as undergraduate at Cambridge that he was deemed fit recipient for a dedicatory notice, as Lettsom, with Thackeray, was one of the writers in the short-lived university paper called "The Snob." We can imagine the sparkling sentences which would have surged up as a record of that old time. But strange to say the honor was declined, and this spurning of immortality became a personal loss to most people. There is no dedication to the "Book of Snobs" in consequence.

I was in Paris when the first numbers of "Vanity Fair" came out, and like the equally immortal "Pickwick Papers," the preliminary chapters were not accepted with the enthusiasm accorded to the future developments. Toward the closing months, on my return to England, and in rambles in the evening from Young Street, accompanied by Thackeray, and others, the talk was generally not alone about the prodigious success already achieved, but as to the probable dénouement of the story. It was Thackeray's humor to baffle enterprising inquisitiveness by evolving different lines and modes of winding up the career of Becky, Dobbin, and the others, having doubtless already well settled mentally how they were finally to be allotted their dues. One exceptional instance I remember in which a suggestion was accepted as valuable. It occurred in June, 1848, one day when Thackeray came at lunch-time to my father's Hampstead house. Torrens McCullagh, happening to be one of the party, said across the table to Thackeray, "Well, I see you are going to shut up your puppets in their box!" His immediate reply was, "Yes; and, with your permission,

I 'll work up that simile." How skilfully
that chance phrase was worked up in the
prefatorial "Before the Curtain," all his
readers well know.

About this time — it may be two or three
months previous — De Noé, the illustrator of
French manners and customs, came over to
England, and was hospitably entertained at
Young Street. Though I did n't meet him
here at this time, he was an old chum at the
Delaroche atelier. Like Thackeray, though
assiduous for a while at the class for drawing,
he only assimilated enough skill for carrying
out his fertile grotesque delineations chiefly
in the pages of "Punch's" precursor, the
French "Charivari." His parody of the an-
nual salons was always delightfully comic,
and the recipients of his good-humored chaff
were the first to join in the laugh.

Quite the opposite in character was M.
Louis Marvy, who was welcomed to Thack-

eray's home at Kensington during his short
sojourn, as related in the "Landscape Painters of England," the materials for which he
got together here. These were a score of
mezzotint etchings executed in the manner
known in France as *vernis mou*, in which he
was an adept. Thackeray had obtained the
permission of noble owners of galleries to
single out specimens of English masters
from their collections, and when done of-
fered the prints to a publisher. The latter
only consented conditionally on Thackeray
himself furnishing the text for them. A se-
vere illness at this critical time laid Thackeray prostrate, and the "Pendennis" monthly
issues were stopped for four months by a
bilious fever. When he rallied, however,
with wonderful powers of recuperation, we
were delighted to note that his former vigor-
ous appetite had returned. He even went
so far as to declare that the dish of roast-pig

with its crackle coating, of which he with relish partook at my father's table, had given the finishing touch to his convalescence.

His first benevolent thought on recovery was to fulfil his contract with the printer, so as to endeavor to help the replenishing of Marvy's coffers. With this object he wrote to me, on November 7, 1849, the following letter:

KENSINGTON, Wednesday.

MY DEAR EYRE

Come to me as soon as pawsable, and let us work off that set of texts for Bogue. I think I could dictate some and you could supply more, and we could be soon done with the dem bugbear.

Ever yours   W. M. T.

Come in the earliest morning you can to breakfast; bring the plates with you and let us go to work.

I went next morning as requested. Thackeray began with the first plate, that of Turner (also the most important one), preparing

Kensington. Wednesday.

My dear Eyre

Come to me as soon as pausable, and let us
knock off that set of texts for Vogue. I think I could
dictate some and you could supply more and we
could be soon done with the dern business.

Ever yours   Holmes.

Come in the earliest morning you can to
breakfast; bring the plates with you & let us
go to work,

paragraphs full of discriminating phraseol-
ogy, with a dash of banter at the later phases
of the painter's career, which seems to me
even now the perfection of a brief summing
up of noble qualities, and equal to the subject in hand.   As the others followed, it af-
forded me an opportunity of assisting at the
welding operation, by which fragmentary
sentences of my own became fluent prose,
and mere matter of fact was enlivened as if
by a magic pen.

        .

When I recently finished my drawing of
the Kensington house, I strolled down the
well-known street in search of rest in the
greenery of Kensington Gardens — a grateful
relief to the eyes after dwelling upon the
sullen colors of old brick-work.   Vast piles
have arisen in the neighborhood, forming a
medley of stores, houses, and hotels which

cater to the wants of the ever-increasing population of the once courtly suburb.

Following this period, No. 36 Onslow Square, for ten years or more, was the next of the author's homes; and there, on the second floor, was the study in which so many well-known tales, essays, romances, lectures, etc., were written. They are all enumerated in Mr. Shepherd's useful Bibliography of the author. The house, with its portico, its balcony, iron framed, even the smaller top windows near the coping, recalls structurally those found in older London squares, which doubtless served as models for these later imitations. A recently published volume, Dr. Shirley's pleasant "Table Talk," tells us of an interview in this "den" with the writer, at that time looking worn and ill. The den, so called, was a most cheerful one; its windows commanded a view of the old avenue of elm-trees. The walls

House at No. 36 Onslow Square, Brompton.

were decked with woodland water-color
scenes by his favorite, Mr. Bennett, and quite
in a central place was the beautiful mezzotint print of Sir Joshua's "Little Girl in the
Snow," a playful terrier and robin redbreast
as her companions. As a change he would
at times prefer the ground-floor room, and
dictate while lounging on an ottoman—too
often battling with pain in later days. The little bronze statuette of George IV. on the man-
telpiece had the look of an ironical genius
loci, when the work of hammering out the
lectures of the Four Georges was on the anvil.

Connected with these a little digression
may be here permissible. He gave these
lectures at Cupar, Fife, among other locali-
ties. Happening to stroll along one of the
principal thoroughfares of that town—Cross
Gate—he was tickled at seeing an emblem-
atic picture over the doorway of the "Battle
of Waterloo" Inn.

"What," he exclaims, in his "Small Beer
Chronicle," in the "Cornhill Magazine" of
July, 1861, "what do you think the sign is?
The 'Battle of Waterloo' is one broad
Scotchman laying about him with a broad-
sword." Happening to be in Cupar I
sketched it, as here shown. Local tradition
has it that a veteran Highlander, of the name
of Kennedy, Sergeant in the Seventy-ninth
Regiment, who survived the slaughter of that
day, sat for the portrait here reproduced. He
was for many years the Governor of Cupar
jail. I was mortified, on seeing the sign at a
later date, to find that panel painting altered,
as shown in another outline.

In the year 1861 the firm of Jackson &
Graham built for Thackeray the beautiful
brick house at No. 2 Palace Green, Kensington, which alone of all his homes has
the privileged Society of Arts oval com-
memorative tablet inserted in its wall, an-

The original sign over Waterloo Tavern.

Waterloo Tavern, as described by Thackeray in the "Cornhill
Magazine" of July, 1861.

Present Sign over Waterloo Tavern.

Waterloo Tavern as it is To-day.

Drawn from photograph.

nouncing that he here lived and died. An old house stood on its ground when he purchased the site; but after mature consideration he wisely gave up the notion of patching that up with additions, and instead razed the old walls and built up the new. I recollect with what mingled feelings I trod upon its mortar- and brick-bestrewed floors for the first time; it seemed so much too vast for comfort; and how this impression was reversed, when on its completion he invited friends to a housewarming. These warm admirers had to be divided into two sections, as the rooms, though as yet barely furnished, couldn't hold all the invited guests in one lot. This housewarming took place on February 24 and 25, 1862, when our host's play of the "Wolves and the Lamb" was admirably acted by amateurs, those I recollect being the daughters of Sir Henry Cole, Mrs. Caulfield, Follett-Synge, Quinten

Twiss, and Thackeray himself; he, in dumb show, dressed as a pastor blessing the assembled actors at the close of the performance, which was much applauded. My modest contribution was a painting of Mrs. Milliken as she leans upon her harp, an adaptation from an outline illustration in "Lovel the Widower," the novel founded upon this two-act play afterward.

In this house Thackeray was actually placed astride the two parishes of Westminster and Kensington; the boundary line of both running discreetly into the lawn at the back, where a stone denoting the division has been placed.

Thackeray was always a great lover of bric-à-brac shops, the glitter of old silver enticing him to look in at the windows; and ample scope was given in this house for gathering together valuables to fill his rooms.

Not satisfied always with the places as-

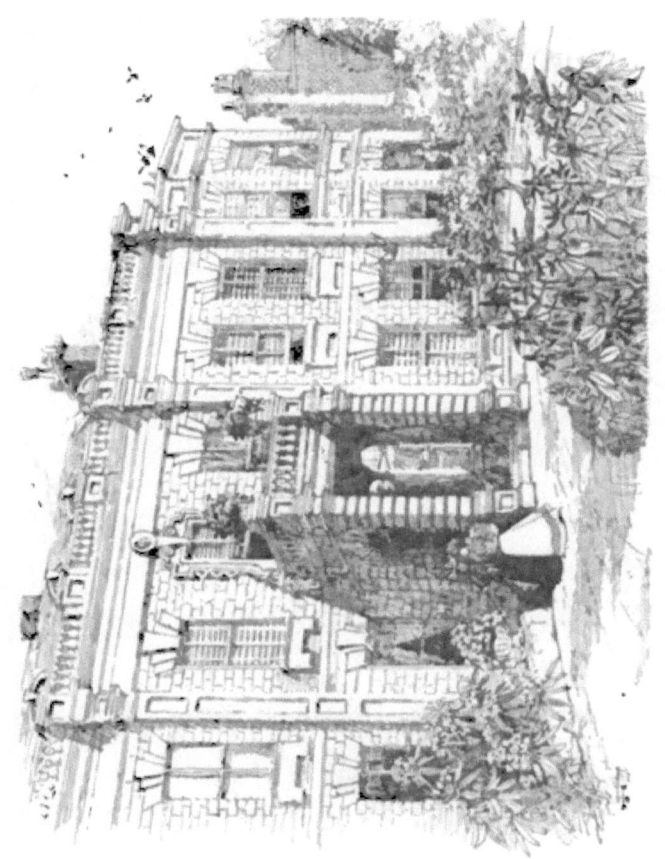

Thackeray's Last House at No. 2 Palace Green, Kensington.

signed to his antiquated pottery, it was one
of his fitful hobbies to search for fresh nooks
to store them in — a glittering vase orna-
mented with cauliflowers being given special
attention. Two Sèvres sauce-boats also were
favorites, and were purchased at the sale of his
effects, on April 1, 1864, for the South Kensington Museum. A large gilt Italian mirror was
purchased at the same time for the museum.

As I look at this handsome dwelling I not
only think of the author's noble presence, so
soon snatched away after a too brief realiza-
tion of its comforts. It also keeps alive the
fond memory of a sister, Amy, whom he so
nobly befriended, who was married from this
home to Thackeray's kinsman, Colonel Ed-
ward Thackeray, V. C. She succumbed to
the trying Indian climate.

Besides his own immediate homes, Thackeray, as all know who follow his descriptive

peregrinations, sought relaxation in what might be called his second homes, the clubs —of which the Garrick and the Reform Club and the Athenæum were the three principal favorites. The immortal Foker has been singled out' as a well-known figure at the first-named one, and others doubtless recognized their photographic likenesses in "Club Snobs"; but the banter was always playful, and added to the popularity of the realistic limner whenever he merely gossiped or dined or joined the evening smoking-groups.

An instance of his kindness of thought, among many, occurs to my mind. Professor Fawcett, not yet M. P., but evidently contemplating a proximate election for some lucky borough, took the initiative step for a Liberal candidate, and joined the Reform Club. He was sitting solitary at lunch-time, and, in his blindness, only hearing an indistinct hum of voices around him. Thackeray, seeing this, beckoned to Bernal Osborne, asking him to come and cheer him up. " I don't know him," was the reply; but soon the three notable and quaintly contrasted personalities were to be seen forming an interesting group. On another occasion Thackeray had invited a young friend to dine with him at the Reform, a day or two before departing for India. His guest appeared emerging out of a cab, without a hat, which he considered an encumbrance, and stated he had gone about London all day without headgear. This amused our host, who grinned and muttered at the end of our repast, "Hatless," as if this would work up as a future character in a novel.

I recall several curious slips of the pen which repeated editions of Thackeray's works have failed to correct. These only prove that he, too, was mortal. An instance may be cited from the "Irish Sketch-Book." In the middle of Stephen's Green stands the equestrian statue thus described in Thackeray's pages: "In the whole of Stephen's Green I think there were not more than two nursery-maids to keep company with the statue of George I., who rides on horseback in the middle of the garden, the horse having its foot up to trot, as if he wanted to go out of town too." Of course Thackeray's remonstrance is here directed at the exclusive shutting up of the gardens. But everybody can now enter, and this enables you to read the inscription on the statue, Giorgio Secundo. Why not alter the number in Thackeray's book now that we can do so?

On Tuesday, December 21, 1863, Thackeray attended as a mourner at the last rites of a relative, Lady Rodd. He came afterward and sat down, possibly to write words

Stranger's Room, Reform Club, London, showing portrait of Thackeray by Samuel Laurence, and busts of Sir William Molesworth and Charles Buller.

of condolence, at a favorite seat at the writing-table of the Lower Room of the Reform Club. His extreme pallor struck me as unusual with him, as in spite of pain his face seldom appeared bloodless. Thus seen, with his silvery locks, against the somber array of Parliamentary volumes behind him on the shelves, his noble, massive countenance took on the air of a classical antique bust. For nearly twenty-three years (he having been elected a member in March, 1840) he had often sat down here grasping the pen which was so soon to drop from his hands. Three days after, on the day before Christmas, came the announcement of his death, terrible in its suddenness to those, like myself, who had only his countless benefactions to dwell upon.

A post of honor was afterward assigned, in what is called the "Stranger's Room" of the Reform Club, to an admirable likeness of him done by his friend Samuel Laurence, from studies made when he was making his famous crayon life-size drawings. This portrait was appropriately placed between busts of two of his distinguished Parliamentary friends, Sir William Molesworth and Charles Buller. Immediately beneath was long to be seen the accessory, so usual in old days, of a sarcophagus-cellaret — in its empty condition suggestive of bygone festivity and hospitalities of his own, of which this room was often the actual scene.

www.ingramcontent.com/pod-product-compliance
Lightning Source LLC
Chambersburg PA
CBHW020039030726
47499CB00007B/2499